BUM GANG

OAH

JENNIFER

LUDO

JAMIE

.IP

Also Available:

THE BARE BUM GANG AND
THE FOOTBALL FACE-OFF

THE BARE BUM GANG BATTLE
THE DOGSNATCHERS

THE BARE BUM GANG AND
THE VALLEY OF DOOM

www.barebumgang.com

THE BARE BUM GANG

and the
The Holy Grail

ANTHONY McGOWAN

Illustrated by Frances Castle

RED FOX

THE BARE BUM GANG AND THE HOLY GRAIL
A RED FOX BOOK 978 1 862 30389 8

First published in Great Britain by Red Fox,
an imprint of Random House Children's Books
A Random House Group Company

This edition published 2009

1 3 5 7 9 10 8 6 4 2

Text copyright © Anthony McGowan, 2009
Illustrations copyright © Frances Castle, 2009

The right of Anthony McGowan to be identified as the author
of this work has been asserted in accordance with the
Copyright, Designs and Patents Act 1988.

The Random House Group Limited supports the Forest Stewardship Council
(FSC), the leading international forest certification organization. All our titles
that are printed on Greenpeace-approved FSC-certified paper carry the
FSC logo. Our paper procurement policy can be found at
www.rbooks.co.uk/environment.

Set in Bembo MT Schoolbook 15/20pt
by Falcon Oast Graphic Art Ltd.

Red Fox Books are published by Random House Children's Books,
61–63 Uxbridge Road, London W5 5SA

www.**kids**at**randomhouse**.co.uk
www.**rbooks**.co.uk

Addresses for companies within The Random House Group Limited
can be found at: www.randomhouse.co.uk/offices.htm

THE RANDOM HOUSE GROUP Limited Reg. No. 954009

A CIP catalogue record for this book is available
from the British Library.

Printed and bound in Great Britain by
CPI Bookmarque, Croydon, CR0 4TD

To Patrick Hayes,
godchild extraordinaire

Chapter One

KING ARTHUR

I was in the park with Noah, trying to get the walkie-talkies to work. Getting walkie-talkies to work is one of the most difficult things in the world to do – about as hard, on average, as strangulating a crocodile with your bare hands, or eating a fried egg without getting a dribble of yolk down the front of your jumper. However, as leader of the Bare Bum Gang, doing impossible things such as strangulating crocodiles, etc., was part of my job.

Noah was on one side of the park, and I was on the other. 'Come in, Blue Baboon.

Are you receiving me?'

Blue Baboon was Noah's secret code-name.

'No,' yelled Noah. 'But I can hear you anyway. And if you call me Blue Baboon again, Ludo, I'm going home.'

Noah didn't like being called Blue Baboon, because some baboons have blue bottoms, so he thought it meant that I was calling him a baboon's bum.

I'd changed the batteries, fiddled with all the switches and dials, and bashed the walkie-talkies on the floor for a while, but it made no difference. We might as well have been talking into our shoes.

It was then that I saw the tramp. Our town only had one proper tramp. I didn't know his real name, but everyone called him King Arthur, because he used to wear armour like one of the Knights of the Round Table. Of course, his armour wasn't real. He'd made it himself. The breastplate was a biscuit tin, his helmet was a paint can, his shield was a car hubcap, and for his lance he had a mop handle.

Some people said King Arthur was a loony. That was wrong for two reasons. The first is that you shouldn't call people loonies even if they are, in fact, as crazy as a coot, because it may hurt their feelings. Secondly, I didn't think that King Arthur *was* a loony.

Being a tramp is a very hard job, and if I were a tramp, I'd probably pretend that I was a Knight of the Round Table as well, to take my mind off how rubbish my life was. So, my theory was that he didn't *believe* he was a Knight of the Round Table, he just *pretended* to be one, as a game.

Miss Bridges says that I've got something called a Vivid Imagination, and it's probably the same with King Arthur.

We often used to see him wandering around, looking in the bins in the park for items of interest, or sitting outside Sainsbury's with his helmet in his lap, asking people politely if they had any spare change. My dad always gave him a pound, and I was allowed to put it in his helmet.

Normally King Arthur walked in a shuffly way, because his shoes were broken and flappy and tied together with string, and maybe also because he had bad legs. But now I saw that he was trying to run, which was hard for him. And he was holding the shield over his head. Then I saw why he was running.

The Dockery Gang.

Not all of them, just Dockery, Stanton and Larkin. They were behind King Arthur, laughing and jeering.

And throwing stones.

Now, don't get me wrong — throwing stones is one of my favourite things to do in the world, but not at helpless old people.

Or at your next-door neighbour's windows, unless it was only an accident, and anyway I was aiming at a tin can on top of our fence, and it was completely unfair that I lost ten weeks' pocket money to pay for it.

Seeing poor King Arthur being attacked like that made me very angry. Even Dockery had never sunk this low before. Without even thinking I ran over to them.

'Stop it, you stupid idiots,' I yelled out.

I know I should have thought of something more rude and funny than *idiots*, but I was just too furious.

Dockery paused halfway through throwing a stone, and looked at me. His face went from laughing, to blank, to smiling wickedly.

'What's it got to do with you?'

'I just want you to stop.'

'Ha! And what if I don't want to? What are you going to do about it, cry all over us? That'll really hurt.'

Larkin and Stanton guffawed, which is a special kind of laugh for idiots.

'Me? I won't do anything about it,' I replied calmly. 'But I know someone who will.'

By this time Noah had come up beside me. He was about as much use in a fight as a wet lettuce (actually, even *I* was only about as much use as a dry lettuce, but that's not the point).

Dockery stopped guffawing.

'Noah,' I said, without taking my eyes from Dockery.

'Yes?'

'Call Jennifer on the walkie-talkie. Tell her to get over here pronto. Tell her to put on her karate outfit – she's got some butts to kick.'

Jenny was the girl in our gang. Even though I originally didn't want her to join, I now thought that every gang should have a girl in it. Just one, though. You don't really want more than one girl per gang, because then you'll be in a girl gang, which is one of the worst kinds of gang to be in. Before you know it you'll be neck-deep in Barbie dolls and My Little Ponies and perfume and flowers.

But one girl is perfect, especially if she's Jenny. The thing is that Jenny is brilliant at karate, tae kwon do, judo and kung fu, and is quite capable of kicking the butts of Dockery and his gang without breaking a sweat.

'But – but . . .' stammered Noah.

'Just do it.'

Then he got it.

'Oh, yes, of course.'

He twisted a dial and pressed a knob.

'Jenny, are you receiving me? Over.'

Then a pause, while he pretended to listen.

'Yes,' he continued. 'We have a *situation* here.'

Another pause. More pretend listening.

'You'll be right over? Great. And you'll

bring the Ninja Death Stars? Excellent.'

And then all we could see were the backs (and butts) of Dockery, Stanton and Larkin as they ran for their lives.

Chapter Two

THE SMELLY GOOD DEED

I was so pleased with our trick that it took me a few seconds to remember King Arthur. I looked around and for a moment I thought he'd gone, flapping away in his flappy shoes. But then I saw a heap on the floor and realized it was him.

Noah saw him too. 'It's the tramp,' he said. 'I think he needs help.'

We ran over to where he was lying. It didn't look too good. King Arthur was on his back with his eyes shut and his mouth open. It didn't smell too good, either. I know it's hard keeping fresh and clean when you're

a tramp, but King Arthur was one of the smelliest tramps around. On a scale of one to ten, where one is having a sniff of a nice flower and ten is having your nose stuck right up a skunk's bum, King Arthur was about a nine point seven.

'Is he dead?' asked Noah, fearfully.

'I don't think so. Usually when you die, your eyes are all starey wide open, like this.' I did an impression of a starey-eyed dead person.

'Then why isn't he breathing?'

Noah sounded like he was on the verge of tears. Noah was easily my best friend, but he definitely spent too much time on the verge of tears. I kept meaning to have a word with him about it, but it would only make him cry if he thought people were talking behind his back about how much he cried.

I looked more carefully at King Arthur. I'd never seen him this close up before. His helmet had fallen off and rolled away on to the grass. He had a beard and long hair, which looked just right for a Knight of the Round Table, except it was all greasy and dirty. I could see a couple of teeth, which was all he had left. One was at the top on the left and the other was at the bottom on the right, which must have been really annoying.

Noah seemed to be right – I couldn't see him breathing at all. I poked him.

'Excuse me, Mr, er, King Arthur. Are you OK?'

Nothing. Not even a twitch.

'You're going to have to give him the kiss of life,' I said to Noah.

'Why me?' he wailed.

'Well, you're the doctor.'

That was true. Noah was our official Gang Doctor. He carried dock leaves around for when we got stung by nettles, and if we got a grass cut he would wee on it for you to stop you getting gangrene, which is when a cut goes bad and your whole body turns into a disgusting gloopy mess, like porridge, and you die in terrible agony.

'But I don't know how to do the kiss of life, not properly. I've only seen it on the telly. I might do it wrong. I might suck when I'm supposed to blow. And anyway,' he said, finally beginning to cry, 'he's so smelly. I know it's not his fault and it's hard being a tramp, but I think I'd be sick in his mouth, and that would only make things worse.'

It was time for me to be a leader.

'Right then,' I said, in my most grown-up

voice. 'You run to Mrs Cake's house and ask her to phone for an ambulance. I'll stay here and . . . and . . . see what I can do.'

Mrs Cake lived in a bungalow next to the park. She had a nasty little dog called Trixie, who used to like chasing us. But I didn't think Trixie would attack, not when we were on a mission to save the life of King Arthur. Only the most evil dogs in the world, such as Hitler's dog, Attila the Hun's dog, or Zoltan – Hound of Dracula, would attack a boy on a mercy mission. Also, Trixie was the girlfriend of our Gang Dog, Rude Word, so she would probably spare Noah because of that.

Without saying anything else, Noah ran off. I think he was glad to have a useful job that didn't involve being too close to the tramp.

I looked down at King Arthur again. If you half-closed your eyes he really did look like a king, with his beard and long hair. And here he was, dying, right in front of me.

Well, I couldn't let that happen. Noah might not know how to do the kiss-of-life, but I did. My scout group did a lesson in Artificial Respiration, using a special Kiss-of-Life dummy called Doris. I ran through what we'd learned.

First, you check the mouth for obstructions, which means twigs, rocks, mice, vomit, puke, etc. Then you lift up their neck and sort of shove their head back. Then you squeeze their nose, and only then are you allowed to blow into their mouth. Or something like that.

I knelt down beside the tramp.

Close up, the stink was even worse. In school we'd been doing the Victorians, and they had something called The Great Big Stink, which was because all the poo and general yuckiness of London went into the River Thames and it whiffed so badly that millions of people died from the sheer rottenness of it, and the rest of them ran away to India, Africa, etc., etc., and invented the British Empire.

Well, as bad as The Great Big Stink stank, it probably didn't smell as bad as King Arthur, up close.

But that didn't matter. He was a human being, just like you or me or the Queen, and he deserved to live. Holding my breath, I got ready to deliver the kiss of life.

I had just begun to open his mouth to check for the twigs, mice, etc., when one of King Arthur's bloodshot eyes opened.

'Who the heck are you?' he spluttered.

It was such a shock I thought I was going to have a heart attack, and then *he* would have had to give *me* the kiss of life.

'Oh, sorry, I thought you were dying.'

King Arthur opened his other eye. 'We're all dying,' he said, 'from the day we're born.'

'You sound like my friend The Moan,' I said.

He pushed himself up on one elbow, but then flopped down again.

'Are you OK?' I asked.

'Fine, fine,' he said. 'Just need to rest my eyes for a minute.'

His eyelids drooped.

'My friend's gone to call for an ambulance,' I said, trying to reassure him.

It had the opposite effect. His eyes pinged open again and he tried to get up.

'No doctors. Doctors kill you sure as anything. If they put me in that hospital I'll never get out alive!'

'It'll be fine,' I said. 'They'll look after

you – they'll give you a comfy bed and nice dinners so you won't have to sleep on a bench or eat rubbish out of the bins any more.'

Then, in the distance, I heard the sound of the ambulance siren. I looked up and saw the ambulance on the track leading up to the park. From the other direction I saw Noah running. He'd done well.

King Arthur sat up and grabbed my arm. His nails were like long black claws. Suddenly I was slightly afraid.

I tried to pull away, but the tramp gripped me like an eagle with its talons in its prey.

'Boy,' he hissed. 'Listen to me. Listen good, before they get here. I've a treasure. A special thing. A magical thing. It's in my place. My place in the high tower.'

Then King Arthur let go of me, and pointed with his bony finger. The place he pointed to was a ruined block of flats called Corbin Tower. It had once been bright and shiny and new, but now most of the windows were broken and the concrete was the colour of dead fish, and it stood in the middle of a wasteland. There was a high, barbed-wire fence all around it. No one was supposed to live there. In fact it was about to be blown up to make way for a new leisure centre and luxury apartments.

'But you can't live there,' I said. 'I've heard there are wild dogs and giant rats and all kinds of other scary stuff. My dad told me there are monsters and ghouls too, but that's just to stop us from trying to play there.'

'Monsters? Ghouls? Aye, maybe, maybe,' said King Arthur, his voice rasping and rattling like chains being dragged over gravel. 'But listen now, boy. You go, top floor. You bring me back my precious thing. You bring it. Swear to me.'

And King Arthur gripped me tighter and pulled me close, so his face filled my vision, and I could smell his graveyard breath.

And I could not stop myself from answering, 'Yes.'

But again King Arthur said, 'You swear? On your life?'

'On my life,' I said, my voice barely a murmur.

Chapter Three

THE QUEST

At that moment the paramedics from the ambulance arrived, a man and a lady wearing green uniforms.

Noah, panting, was right behind them.

'He's alive!' he yelled delightedly. 'I thought he was a gonner.'

'Charming,' said King Arthur.

The paramedics had a special wheely stretcher that went down low so they could put the tramp on, and then high again so they could push it to the ambulance.

The lady paramedic said, 'Well done, boys. You did exactly the right thing.'

I nearly asked if there was a reward for saving tramps, old people, etc., etc., but I stopped myself in case the nice ambulance lady thought that we only did it for the money.

Noah and I were feeling quite pleased as we watched the ambulance drive away. It's exactly what the Bare Bum Gang was all about – saving lives, I mean. That, and eating sweets, crushing our enemies, throwing stones in puddles, etc.

Noah told me that he'd called the others as well, so I thought this might be a good time for a gang feast.

At that moment something made me turn round, and I saw Larkin lurking behind the broken seesaw. Dockery must have told him to hide and spy on us. I wondered if he was close enough to have heard what King Arthur had said.

When he saw that we were looking at him, he ran away, although that might have been because the rest of the gang had just appeared – the rest of the gang being Jenny, her brother Phillip, and Jamie.

We usually called Phillip 'The Moan', because there was nothing he wouldn't moan about. If you gave him a bag with a million pounds in it, he would complain about it being too heavy, or he would say it was the wrong sort of bag. Technically, The Moan was our Gang Admiral, although we didn't actually have a navy yet.

We only ever called Jenny Jenny (or sometimes Jennifer), because if we called her anything else, such as Silly Cow, Duck Face, Monkey Bum, Stinky Cheese Girl, etc., etc., she'd have kicked us all into next week, and not even the beginning of next week, such as Monday or Tuesday, but half past eleven on Sunday night.

Jamie was our Gang General, because he was brave and not very clever. If you were being mean about him, you'd say that each time he counted on his fingers he came to a different number. If you were being kind, you'd say that he was never wrong by more than two.

'What's been going on?' asked Jenny.

'Important things,' I replied importantly. 'Too important to talk about here, where spies are lurking. Let's go to the den and I'll tell you the whole story. I promise, you won't be disappointed.'

Our gang den was probably the finest ever constructed in the history of the world. It was partly tunnelled into the side of a hill, and the entrance was disguised by a weeping willow tree. We had lots of traps around it to deter our enemies (chiefly Dockery and his gang), the best of which was probably our famous Smarties-Tube Fart-Bomb trap. It was the traps that stopped the Dockery Gang from sneaking up on our den in order to conquer it, smash it in, wee in it, etc., etc.

When we were all safely inside the den, and munching away on sweets from the sweet stash (mainly jelly worms, with a few wine gums and cola bottles for variety), Noah and I told the others all about saving the tramp.

'Would you really have given him the kiss of life?' Jenny asked, in awe.

I nodded. I felt like someone who'd heroically given up his life, even though I hadn't really given up anything, which was pretty cool.

'Disgusting!' moaned Jamie, making puking gestures by pretending to stick

his fingers down his throat.

'I think it's brave and wonderful,' said Jenny, which made me blush.

To stop everyone noticing the blushing business, I quickly told them about King Arthur's treasure.

'What do you think it is?' asked Jamie. 'Money?'

'It might be pieces of eight and gold doubloons and jewels,' said Jenny.

'More like old tramp rubbish,' said The Moan. 'Tin cans and mouldy newspapers

and a half-eaten sausage roll he's found in a bin.'

'I think you're all wrong,' I said. 'I don't think it's valuable in the way money and jewels are valuable. And I don't think it's just loony tramp rubbish either. I think it's something out of the ordinary – something . . . amazing.'

Noah gasped, Jenny sighed, The Moan tutted, and Jamie blew a spit bubble.

Then Noah said, 'What were his exact words?'

I thought hard, trying to remember. 'He said, "I've a treasure. A special thing. A magical thing."'

'So he did *definitely* say treasure?' Jenny asked.

'Yes, I think so.'

'So it could *easily* be jewels? Emeralds and rubies and sapphires?'

'Well, maybe. But I just don't think he meant that kind of treasure. I think it was something more – oh, I don't know, *important* than mere emeralds and gold doubloons.'

'There's nothing *mere* about gold doubloons and emeralds,' said The Moan. 'With that sort of treasure, *real treasure*, I mean, you can buy anything you want. You could buy Chelsea Football Club, and then sack all the players and buy rubbish players and make them play so Chelsea lost every match, like they ought to.'

In case you hadn't realized, The Moan didn't like Chelsea very much.

'Or you could help to save the poor people in Africa,' added Noah.

Noah often talked about helping the poor people in Africa, partly because his great-great-great-great-great-great-granny and granddad came from there, but also because he was nice.

'Or you could buy some really good sticks,' said Jamie.

Jamie liked sticks.

'Don't be stupid,' said The Moan. 'Why would you buy sticks? You can find sticks anywhere, for free. You might as well buy leaves or . . . or dog poo.'

'I don't want any dog poo. And I was talking about special sticks.'

'What kind of special sticks?'

'I dunno. Gold ones, maybe.'

That seemed to satisfy The Moan. He could see the point of buying some gold sticks.

'Look,' I said, 'I don't think this is going to be a pirate type of adventure with treasure and pieces of eight and golden sticks. I think this is going to be an adventure from the days of knights and chivalry. Remember, we're talking about King Arthur's special thing. And what was the original King Arthur's special thing?'

'His big sword, what-do-yer-call-it? Ex-scabby-butt,' said Jamie. 'Or is it Ex-halibut?'

'A halibut is a flat fish,' said Noah. 'I think you mean Excalibur.'

'Yeah, that,' said Jamie.

He swished about in the air as if he were wielding Excalibur. Or perhaps it was one of his special golden sticks.

'That would actually be quite cool, if it were true,' said The Moan. He pretended to fight with Jamie, both using invisible swords.

'I didn't mean the sword,' I said. 'I was thinking of the Graily Hole. No, I mean the Holy Grail.'

'That's just a fairy story,' said The Moan.

'And what exactly is a grail anyway?' asked Jenny.

'A grail? Well, it's some kind of a holy thing. I think it might be a cup. Or a plate.'

'Or a teapot?' said Jamie.

'No, definitely not a teapot. They didn't have teapots in the time of knights.'

'Sounds rubbish,' said The Moan.

'But I don't think it matters exactly what King Arthur's treasure is. I made a promise, and our mission is clear. We have to find the tramp's old lair at the top of Corbin Tower in the wasteland, get the treasure and bring it back for him.'

'I don't quite see how it has to be *our* mission,' said The Moan. 'I don't want to go to that spooky old tower even if there is real treasure in it.'

'It does sound quite dangerous,' added Noah.

'And there are the giant rats and . . . other things,' said Jamie, although he didn't sound too bothered. The only thing Jamie was afraid of was custard. If it even touched his bowl he'd start crying and go off to hide in a corner.

'For once I think Phillip is right,' said Jenny. That was a bit of a shock. Jenny never agreed with anything The Moan said. 'But not because of that nonsense about monsters. I read in the paper that they're finally going to demolish Corbin Tower on Monday.'

'Monday!' I exclaimed. 'That means we

only have one more day to get the Holy Grail—'

'Or emeralds,' chipped in Jamie.

'You're not seriously still going to go in, are you?' asked The Moan, shaking his head.

'I made a promise,' I replied. 'And you're right. I can't ask you to come with me. It is too dangerous. There are unimaginable perils awaiting whoever attempts this quest, including giant rats, wild dogs, maybe some poisonous snakes, evil dwarfs, quicksand, etc., etc., all ending in a gigantic explosion bigger than when an asteroid crashed to earth and killed every single dinosaur in the world in a second. No, I can't ask you to come. I'll go alone.'

There was a silence after that, while everyone appreciated my amazing bravery, gumption, pluck, etc. I could sense Jenny's admiration, bathing me like radiation from a nuclear power station core, except good radiation rather than bad.

The silence was broken by Noah.

'I'll come,' he said quietly. Some people might say that Noah was the most cowardly member of the Bare Bum Gang, just because he cried quite a lot, but I knew deep down he was probably really brave – the second bravest, in fact, after me. Well, maybe third, if you include Jamie, except that I'm not sure if you should include him, because his bravery was connected to him being a bit thick.

In fact, Jamie was the next to speak.

'Me too,' he said. 'I'm not afraid of rats. Or getting blown up.'

See what I mean?

'Well, if you're all going, I'll go too,' said Jenny.

I smiled at her and she smiled back.

That just left The Moan.

He fiddled about with his shoelaces for a while, and then finally said, 'OK, me too. I'm not letting you lot get all the emeralds and rubies, leaving me with nothing but the wine gums.'

That was it. The whole team. Me, Noah, Jamie, The Moan and Jennifer.

Except for one, that is.

Guess who?

We arranged to rendezvous the next day after breakfast, at the vandalized bus shelter near Corbin Tower. I told them all to come fully kitted out for the most dangerous and exciting adventure of our lives.

Chapter Four

AN OLD FRIEND RETURNS

I was the last person to reach the bus stop, the first stage in our quest to recover the Holy Grail for King Arthur. I wasn't last because I was a slowcoach, or because I'd been watching telly, but because I had to go and fetch the final member of the Bare Bum Gang.

'Rude Word!' yelled Jenny when she saw him.

I don't mean that she shouted out any old rude word, such as 'bum', 'fart', or 'poo'.

No, you see, Rude Word, as I've already mentioned, is the name of our Gang Dog.

For reasons *way* too complicated to explain, he lived half the year with me and half the year with someone called Declan, who went to our school but was in a completely different gang called The Commandos.

Now, Rude Word was not one of those pretty dogs with lovely floppy ears and big eyes. Nor was he one of the clever dogs that can do amazing tricks. He couldn't roll over, play dead, fetch a stick or say the word 'sausages' when you moved his mouth up and down like a dog I saw once on the telly. He wasn't any good at finding treasure, and he'd never caught a Frisbee (although he had once eaten one). He was as ugly as a bucket of toads and his only trick was licking his bottom while also scratching his ear.

He only had one, by the way. I mean ear, not bottom. Well, he only had one bottom as well, but that's usual among dogs. And humans. There may be some space aliens that have two or more bottoms, but we haven't discovered them yet, and, actually, I hope we never do.

Anyway, now the summer holidays had started, it was my turn to have Rude Word (or Rudy, as we sometimes called him, because it seemed a bit less rude) again.

When I collected him, Declan looked very sad. However, his mum and dad looked the opposite of sad, by which I mean happy. They were architects and lived in a very posh house, and everything in it was white, except for a few things that were black.

Or at least that was how it used to be before Rude Word got to work on it. He'd eaten big chunks out of most of the furniture, which I'd expected. He also seemed to have eaten most of a wall, half of the DVD player, and the taps in the bathroom. And now, as well as the white and the black, there were quite a few splodges of brown, caused by . . . well, I'm sure I don't have to tell you.

He was very pleased to see me, especially when he saw that I'd brought him a jelly worm. He licked my face, which was a bit like putting my head into a warm toilet, i.e. (or is it e.g.?) not very nice.

Declan had bought him a new collar and lead. The collar had a tag on it engraved with RUDE WORD – which was cool, as that was also his name.

Of the rest of the gang, Jamie was pleased to see Rudy, and The Moan was sort of neutral, like Switzerland in the war. Noah didn't really get on with dogs, but even he tried to smile. He could probably see how useful it might be to have our own trained attack dog when facing monsters, etc.

The bus stop where we met was on the road that went along the edge of the wasteland. The wasteland wasn't always a wasteland. There used to be lots and lots of little houses all squished together. The little houses were knocked down before I was born, and the tower block was built in the middle. The area around the tower was supposed to have been all green and lovely with trees and bushes and playgrounds and tennis courts, but the land turned out to be polluted and poisoned and nothing would grow except weeds and plastic bags. I can still remember when people lived in the tower, but they never looked very happy, and eventually they all moved out, and King Arthur moved in.

Now that the tower block was going to be demolished, the whole area was basically a giant building site with cranes and wrecking balls and dumper trucks and piles of building materials.

We all stood and looked at it now, staring through the wire fence that surrounded the site. The wasteland was as brown and grey as an old man's teeth, and the tower reached into the sky like a bony witch's finger. It had been sunny when we'd all set out, but now the sky was dark and gloomy. Even Rude Word looked depressed. Normally, when he was in a new place, he'd make a point of weeing on everything (and everyone), but now he just made a whining sound, and hugged my leg. I don't suppose I was the only one wishing he (or she, in Jennifer's case) was back at home lying in front of the telly watching cartoons.

'Let's get this done,' I said, trying to sound more hopeful than I felt.

'Have you got a plan?' Noah asked.

'Of course,' I replied. 'But first let's do an equipment check.'

I made everyone unload what was in their packs. Jenny had a hairbrush (useful, she explained, in close hand-to-hand combat), some lip salve (cherry flavour), and a spare thingy for tying her hair up. Jamie had a sausage roll and a scotch egg which he said were dual function – you could eat them, or throw them at your attackers. The Moan had a pack of Top Trump cards ('In case we get bored,' he said), and Noah had his full expedition-grade medical kit.

I had the best gear. I'd brought my new multi-tool, which I'd got for my birthday.

It was really clever, and had lots of useful gadgets hidden away in it, such as: some scissors; a thing for getting stones out of horses' hooves; a magnifying glass; a hammer; some pliers and a (very small) saw – useful for sawing (very small) twigs in half. I also had some string (only my second-best string, in case I lost it), some matches with the heads dipped in melted wax to keep them dry, a harmonica (to play in prison if we got captured), my pen torch, a tube of toothpaste (you can use it to dissolve the bars on prison windows, plus it's good for brushing your teeth with) and, best of all, my German U-boat Captain's binoculars. I knew they were German U-boat Captain's binoculars because that's what the man in the market said when he sold them to my dad. I suppose you could argue that they were evil binoculars, because U-boats used to sink our ships in the war, but you can't really blame the binoculars for that.

Anyway, they were probably the best binoculars in the world, so I didn't mind if they were a little bit evil, say ten to fifteen per cent. It's only when things get to be twenty-five to fifty per cent evil that you should throw them away.

We put our things back in our packs and I led the way along the road to the main gate into the wasteland. Like I said, there was a high fence all around the site.

The bottom part of the fence was just ordinary wire, but the top part was razor wire, which is like barbed wire, but more deadly. It's designed to rip your guts open so your insides, including your liver, kidneys, intestines, stomach, etc., etc., all fall out if you try to climb over it, which I think should be against the law *and* illegal.

The gate was usually locked up with a chain, so you couldn't just push it open. However, it was lower than the fence and, most importantly, there wasn't any razor wire on top to slice your guts open. The top of it was level with my head.

'What now?' asked The Moan.

'We go over,' I replied. 'Give me a leg up, Jamie.'

Jamie was as strong as an ox. Well, a small ox. A baby one. But that's still quite strong, compared to, say, a newt or a rabbit. Without complaining he knelt on all fours and let me climb on his back. It was still a long way up to the top of the gate, but I managed to swing one leg over.

At exactly that moment, a loud voice rang out.

'Oi! You! What do you think you're playing at?'

And with the voice there came a terrifying growling and snarling, as if a Hound of Hell had been loosed upon us.

Jamie collapsed, leaving me dangling with one leg on each side of the gate, which, I can tell you, was not very comfortable.

But that was the least of my problems.

Chapter Five

THE GATEKEEPER

I looked up and saw a man striding towards me. He was dressed like an SS Stormtrooper with a black uniform and a black helmet and big black boots and he was waving a long black truncheon and he looked about as mean as a velociraptor with toothache. He had a badge on his black jacket with a picture of a mailed fist (which isn't actually a fist you post through the mail, but a fist covered in chain mail).

It wasn't the man who'd done the snarling, but the gigantic dog straining at the leash he was holding.

The man had emerged from a little hut with the words GROUP 9 SECURITY written on it, along with a bigger version of the mailed fist from the badge.

I hadn't realized the building site was controlled by Group 9. Group 9 Security were infamous, which is the bad version of famous. It was well known that if they caught you messing about where you shouldn't be, whether on a building site like this, or a car park, or if you were being naughty in the shopping centre, they'd give you a great big kick up the bum and then take you to the police, who'd put you straight in jail and throw away the key.

The Group 9 dogs were even more infamous. It was said that they were given torn-up boys' trousers mixed in with their dog meat to train them to bite you on the bum. It worked like this: *Yum yum yum* (that is the dog thinking, by the way), *this is nice dog meat – not sure about these bits of trouser, though – but wait, let me think . . . I suppose that means that nice dog meat like this lives inside trousers, so all I have to do to get as much nice dog meat as I like is to chew up whoever is wearing trousers, especially if it is a small boy.*

This dog was even uglier than Rude Word, as well as being much bigger. He was dragging the Group 9 Security man as if he was a little child. The dog's lips were curled back, showing his huge fangs, which looked like this:

It was the kind of dog cave men would have used to help them hunt woolly mammoths, woolly rhinoceroses, woolly giant bears, woolly giant killer sheep, etc., etc.

Being a mammoth-eating dog's dinner was not how I wanted to die. I tried to get down off the gate, but it was really hard to swing my leg back over. Jenny was screaming at me, and Noah and The Moan pulled and tugged, which just made things worse. The dog was getting closer and closer, along with the Group 9 man and his nasty truncheon. In the end I just sort of fell off – luckily onto the outside, or I'd have been gobbled up for sure.

The dog threw itself at the fence, barking like a mad thing.

'Down, down,' the man yelled, yanking at the leash.

I looked for Rude Word. He was hiding behind Noah, who was hiding behind The Moan, who was hiding behind Jenny, who was hiding behind Jamie. Jamie had his eyes shut, which he believed made him invisible.

'Can't you kids read?' the man shouted.

'Yes, we can read,' I replied, 'including Jamie, as long as there aren't any big words.'

'Read that then,' he growled, pointing with his truncheon to a big sign that said:

PRIVATE PROPERTY

TRESPASSERS WILL BE PROSECUTED

'Got that? It's dangerous here. There're hazards. Building sites aren't playgrounds. Now clear off.'

'Actually,' I replied calmly, 'we're on the street, which belongs to everyone.'

'Don't you cheek me, you little hooligan. You were climbing over this gate, and don't deny it. And you can thank your lucky stars you never made it, because this dog here hasn't had its dinner yet.'

So, it was true! They really were trained to eat little boys! I gulped.

'I was just trying to get my stick,' I said.

'What stick?'

I looked around. 'That one,' I said, with relief, pointing to a knobbly twig on the other side of the fence.

Now, I like sticks. Not as much as Jamie, but I like them. They're one of the best things for playing with when you haven't got any real toys. And the great thing about a stick is that if you break it in half, you haven't got a broken stick, but two sticks. Cool, eh? Try that with a machine gun or a bazooka.

The Group 9 guy went and picked up the stick. He came back and held it out to me, over the top of the gate. As I was about to take it, he whipped it away and dangled it in front of his dog. The hellhound's eyes lit up, and it clamped down on the poor stick with its deadly jaws and mashed it to bits in seconds. Then it ate the shreds.

Without another word the guard turned round and went back to his little hut, dragging the dog with him. Just as they were disappearing, Rude Word came out of hiding and gave one feeble bark, but when the Group 9 dog turned for a last snarl, he whimpered and hid behind Noah again.

Chapter Six

THE TUNNEL OF DOOM OR DEATH OR SOMETHING

'I never want to see that thing again,' said Noah, still trembling slightly. 'I mean, what kind of dog was it anyway? It didn't look like any species I've ever seen before.'

I was going to tell him my theory about it being a cave-man dog, then it struck me. We were confronted by something way worse than a mere Neanderthal dog. I've already mentioned the list of the world's most evil dogs, and this one was on that list for sure.

'It was Zoltan,' I said, 'feared Hound of Dracula.'

'How do you know?'

'I saw him on the telly when we had a babysitter who let me stay up. It was so scary I made myself forget. But that's definitely him.'

The Bare Bum Gang all nodded solemnly. Now we knew what we were up against: the evil Group 9 security machine, plus Zoltan, Hound of Dracula.

'What now?' said The Moan. 'We can't get over the fence because it's too high, and we can't get over the gate because that dog will eat us, and the guard will shovel up the remains and send them back to our parents in a plastic bag.'

'Maybe we should just go and play in the den,' said Noah.

'I might go to my karate practice,' said Jenny.

Jamie did a large burp.

Rude Word woofed.

For a second I weakened. The guard may have been horrid, but he did have a point about building sites. They can be dangerous places and kids shouldn't really play there. But this was an official quest. We were on a chivalrous mission to save the Holy Grail, or maybe some golden sticks.

I took a deep breath. 'There's another way,' I said.

'In your dreams,' said The Moan.

'Not quite in my dreams,' I replied. 'More like in my nightmares.'

That got their attention.

'Surely,' said Noah, his voice trembling, 'you don't mean . . .'

'That's exactly what I mean.'

'You're crazy,' said The Moan.

Jamie burped again, but this time his meaning was clear: *I think you're mad too.*

'What are you lot talking about?' said Jenny.

'He's talking about the tunnel. The Tunnel of Doom,' said The Moan.

'Hang on,' I said 'I don't think we can really call it the Tunnel of Doom.'

'Why not? It's a tunnel and we're doomed if we go in it.'

'Because we had the Valley of Doom in our last big adventure, and it makes it sound like we've run out of good ideas to call things.'

'Well, what do you suggest then, clever clogs?'

'What about the Tunnel of Terror?'

'No.'

'The Tunnel of Tears?'

'No.'

'The Tunnel of Death?'

'Maybe. Not sure.'

'Tunnel of Poo,' said Jamie, his first words that weren't in burp language for ages.

'That's actually not bad,' said The Moan, 'because in fact that's what it is, a tunnel full of poo.'

'Look,' said Jenny angrily, 'would someone please tell me what you're talking about!'

I looked at her with my most serious face. It was the sort of face you see on the telly when the doctor has to tell someone they only have twenty-four hours to live.

'The Tunnel of Death—'

'Or Poo,' said Jamie.

'The Tunnel of *Whatever* is the old sewer that went to the little houses that used to be where the tower is. There's a place where you can get into it *outside* the fence, and another place where you can get out of it *inside* the fence. It's the only way.'

'But how do you know about it?'

'We used to do it as a dare sometimes. I mean, the dare was to go through the tunnel to the wasteland. But no one ever made it all the way. They always came back after a few metres. It was too foul down there.'

'You always got covered in poo,' said Jamie.

'It wasn't poo,' I snapped. 'Just brown stuff.'

'Yeah,' said The Moan, 'brown stuff that came out of people's bottoms.'

'And you want us to go down the same stinky sewer?' said Jenny, her eyes wide with disbelief. 'Even though no one has ever made it all the way through? You're crackers.'

It was time to take control again.

'None of the kids who failed were on a noble quest like us. Remember, we're like the Knights of King Arthur. I'm Lancelot, The Moan is Sir Gawain, Noah is Sir Galahad, Jamie is Sir . . .' But then I ran out of Sirs.

Luckily Noah came to the rescue.

'Sir Tristan.'

'Exactly, Sir Tristan. And Jennifer is Queen Guinevere.'

'Queen Yuck!' said Jenny. 'I'm the best fighter, so I should be Lancelot.'

'That's not right,' I replied, 'because then I'd have to be Queen Guinevere. Let me think . . . OK, you can be Sir Gawain, Jenny, and The Moan can be Queen Guinevere.'

'No way,' grumbled The Moan. 'If I'm Guinevere I'm definitely going home.'

'Are there any other spare Sirs?' I asked Noah in desperation.

'Sir Bors.'

'Sir Boring! You just made that up. No way I'm being him.'

'He was Lancelot's brother, actually,' said Noah. 'But if it makes you happy, *I'll* be Guinevere, and *you* can be Galahad.'

'That's really noble, Noah,' I said, and I think the whole gang were impressed by his supreme act of self-sacrifice. 'Right,' I continued. 'Now that's settled, let's get on with this quest or we'll never make it home in time for *Doctor Who*.'

'Do you remember where the tunnel is?' Noah asked.

I think that maybe he was hoping I wouldn't.

But I did remember, and I led the gang around the perimeter fence to the right place. Between the road and the fence there was a dry ditch. The opening was in the side of the ditch. You could hardly see it to begin with, as it was covered in weeds and rubbish.

I jumped down into the ditch and scraped away the garbage. There was a rusty metal grate as big as a dustbin lid.

'Help me,' I said, looking up at the others.

Noah jumped down, and together we pulled. It had been opened before, but it still took both of us using every bit of strength we had to make it move. Finally it came away,

revealing the tunnel, stretching before us into the darkness. It was just big enough to crawl through on your hands and knees.

'I'm not going in there,' said Jenny. 'Not for a million pounds.'

'Me neither,' said The Moan. 'It stinks like a badger's bum.'

'I don't like tunnels,' said Jamie. 'What if I get stuck and have to live down there for ever like a rabbit? And I don't even like carrots.'

Rude Word woofed.

'Oh, come on,' I said. 'There's nothing to be scared of.' But I was frightened too.

And then something unexpected happened. Little Noah, famous for not being very brave, and for not liking the dark or smelly things, got down on his hands and knees and crawled into the dark smelly drain.

He looked back over his shoulder. 'You lot coming or not?' he said, and then crawled on without waiting.

The rest of us looked at each other. I think the others were feeling a little ashamed. First Jenny, then Jamie, then The Moan and then Rudy followed Noah into the Tunnel of Terror (I'd decided that was probably the best name for it). I was at the back, which is one of the most dangerous places to be when you're in a tunnel, because of possible attacks from the rear.

Chapter Seven

GOING UNDERGROUND

To begin with all I could see in the gloom was Rude Word's big hairy bottom.

It actually didn't smell that bad — I mean the sewer, not Rude Word's bottom, which usually niffed pretty rotten, despite all the licking he gave it. It hadn't rained for a while, so the bottom was dry. I mean the bottom of the tunnel, not Rude Word's bottom. In fact, to avoid confusion, from now on when I mean Rude Word's bottom, I'll say Rude Word's bottom, and when I mean anyone else's bottom, or the bottom of a tunnel or any other kind of bottom, then I'll just say bottom.

I hope that's clear.

'Everyone OK?' I shouted.

My shout echoed along the tunnel in a most spooky manner.

'Can't see a thing,' came an echoey voice back.

'Let me through,' I said. 'I've got my torch.'

I pushed past Rude Word, The Moan, Jamie and Jennifer. It was a tight squeeze, and I ended up getting a bit stuck with Jennifer – which was pretty embarrassing, I can tell you, especially as there were about three seconds when her lips were squidged up against my cheek. Someone might have said this counted as kissing, but that would be completely unfair, as this was a matter of life and death, not just yucky girly kissing stuff.

Finally I was level with Noah.

'Do you want to go first, with the torch?' he asked.

I looked along the sewer. It was pitch black except for the tiniest blip of light from what must be the exit, miles away, it seemed.

'Mmmmm,' I said, 'I think maybe I should shine the torch over your shoulder, so you can see where you're going. In any underground adventure, the Torch Bearer is the most important position, and they shouldn't be right at the front in case there's a pit or trap or something, or a surprise attack. If anyone falls into a trap it shouldn't be the Torch Bearer. Definitely not. Because then, er, there'd be no one to bear the torch. And no torch to bear. Which would definitely be a disaster. So you carry on being first, as you're more dispensable.'

'Thanks,' said Noah, but I don't think he meant it. In fact I think he was being sarcastic, which was all wrong. Being sarcastic was The Moan's job.

'I don't mean that in a bad way, Noah,' I said reassuringly. 'Being dispensable is

also one of the most important jobs, after being Torch Bearer. And Leader, of course. In fact, in any adventure, underground or overground or in mid-air, you can't get by without the dispensable one. The dispensable one is, er, indispensable. Everyone knows that.'

'Can we get on, please?' said The Moan from behind us. 'I don't want to spend the rest of my life in this blinking hole.'

'Yes, yes,' I said, and gave Noah a little push.

I shone the torch over his shoulder. The walls of the sewer had once been red brick,

but now they were blackened with dried slime and other nasty things. If you got all the tunnels in the world and put them in order of nastiness, this one was definitely in the top five per cent, although it was probably better than a tunnel bored into your brain by a creature that's crawled into your ear.

The next ten minutes was one of the most unpleasant experiences of my life – and remember, I've got a baby sister, so I know all about misery.

Sweat began to run down my face and into my eyes, making them sting. Everything ached – my hands, my knees, my back and my head, every time I bashed it on the roof.

Obviously, The Moan was the first to moan.

'This is rotten,' he said. 'I want to go home.'

'My knees hurt,' said Jenny. 'And I think there's a hole in my tights.'

'You should have worn trousers then, like a normal person,' said The Moan.

'No arguing,' I said. 'If we fight amongst ourselves, the enemy will pick us off one by one.'

That did the trick. There was no more arguing, and everyone kept on crawling forwards. It was hard work, but each time I looked up, the light in front was a tiny bit bigger.

I noticed that every few metres there'd be a sort of side tunnel, smaller than the main sewer. It might have been my imagination, but I thought I heard scuffling, rustling noises coming from them, along with a nasty, musty smell.

Then, suddenly, Noah stopped. I bumped into him, and Jenny bumped into me.

'What's the problem?'

'I heard something.'

'What?'

'Squeaking.'

'You mean like a rusty gate?' I said hopefully.

'No. Not like a gate. Like a . . . like a rat.'

Now, I knew that, in normal circumstances, rats are not very dangerous. However, these were not normal circumstances. These were special circumstances. And in certain special circumstances rats are extremely deadly dangerous. One of those special circumstances is if you corner them. Being cornered changes a rat from a nice peaceful (if dirty and annoying) little fellow into one of the most vicious and lethal beasts in the universe, comparable to a jaguar, T. rex, or saltwater crocodile (which is the scariest sort of crocodile, especially if you're at the seaside).

If you corner them (the rats, I mean, not the crocodiles, although that is also not to be recommended) they leap straight for your neck and rip your throat out, leading to blood spurting everywhere and a horrible death, as bad as, or maybe even worse than, death by burning, drowning, electrocution, being eaten by jaguars, etc., etc.

The other situation in which rats become evil, deadly homicidal maniacs is when you enter what is known as their 'home territory'.

And everyone knows that the home territory of the rat is the sewer.

'Did he say rats?'

That was Jenny, still scrunched up behind me. Now I had turned into a sort of sandwich, with Noah in front and Jenny behind. And there's nothing a rat prefers to eat more than a sandwich, whether it's cheese, ham or boy.

'I don't like rats,' she added unnecessarily.

With my hand shaking just a little bit, I shone the torch ahead.

And there, gleaming back, were two points of evil yellow light.

Noah screamed.

I screamed.

Jenny screamed.

The Moan screamed.

Jamie burped.

Then things got really bad.

More yellow dots.

Equals more eyes.

Equals more rats.

Equals more screaming.

It was now that I had to call on all my qualities as a Leader, i.e., dauntless courage, extreme genius and grace under pressure.

'Rude Word,' I yelled. 'Din-dins.'

I heard a wet snuffling sound from behind, and my fat dog came squeezing up.

'Din-dins', you see, means dinner in doggie

language, and it was the only call Rude
Word ever responded to. I took his ugly mug
in my hands and made my speech.

'Listen, Rudy,' I said, staring deeply into his
poo-coloured eyes. 'I know you let yourself

down badly when you hid from that big nasty dog Zoltan earlier on, but now's your chance to make up for it. Many heroes have been cowardy custards for a while, such as Achilles when he sulked in his tent, but then he lost his temper and marmalized millions of Trojans. And that's what you have to do, except with rodents instead of Trojans. You see, ahead of us there lies an army of killer rats. If we go forwards, they'll tear out our throats and drink our blood, like a horde of zombies and vampire bats—'

'Ooooooooooo,' groaned Jennifer.

'And if we turn our backs on them and run away, they'll probably gnaw through our bums and then eat us from the inside out, until all that's left is a load of skellingtons, with fat rats in the middle of them lying around licking their lips, rubbing their swollen tummies, burping, etc., etc.'

'Ooooooooooo,' groaned everyone.

'So, Rudy,' I continued, 'it's all down to you. Understand?'

All through this speech, Rude Word had been looking at me carefully, expecting me to produce his bowl with his dog meat in it. Now he gave a sort of whining yawn that went like this: 'Yyyaaaaaaaaaaaawwwwwwpppp.'

That meant he was ready.

It was now or never.

I pointed down the tunnel at the yellow rats' eyes, and I repeated, 'Din-dins.'

Rudy looked down the tunnel, then back at me, then down the tunnel again. Then, finally, it sank in.

In his time Rude Word had eaten many things – lumps of our car, lots of furniture, Weetabix, snotty hankies, dead pigeons, small trees, Pot Noodles, cat poo and one pet python (or boa constrictor). Now he was about to add something else to his menu. Without another sound, he shot off along the sewer like an iron ball along the barrel of the cannon on a pirate ship.

The rats didn't know what hit them. One second the eyes were there, glinting evilly.

The next second they went out, as if there'd been a power cut, and all we could hear were terrified squeaks.

I shone the torch down the tunnel. Rude Word was gnashing and snapping and chomping and yomping.

'Quick, everyone,' I shouted, 'let's move before they regroup and attack us from the flanks or up the rear. And tuck your trousers inside your socks so the little monsters can't run up your trouser legs and destroy your undercarriage.'

The gang didn't need to be told twice. We zipped along the rest of the tunnel double quick, following in the wake of the doggie tornado that was Rude Word.

In a couple of minutes we were out, blinking in the sunlight.

I didn't look back down the tunnel. If I had . . . well, I might have seen something interesting. And unpleasant. Very unpleasant.

Chapter Eight

THE WASTELAND

Well, it looked like sunlight when we first emerged blinking into it. In fact it was still miserable and grey, but it dazzled us after the darkness of the sewer.

We crouched down behind a pile of bricks that had once been a wall.

'Well done, gang,' I said. 'Did we all make it?'

I did a quick register to make sure. I didn't want to leave anyone behind in the sewer to be eaten alive by rats.

'Noah?'

'Here.'

'Moan.'

'Here.'

'Jenny?'

'Here, of course. Where else would I be?'

'Rude Word?'

'Woof.'

'Jamie?'

'GROOOUUURRRPPPPP.'

'Please, Jamie, no burping. It might give away our position, plus it's disgusting.'

'Sorry.'

'And you haven't said if you're here yet.'

'What? Oh, here.'

'Thank you. Now, gather round, everyone,

and we'll plan the next stage.'

They all squatted in a half-circle round me. Their faces were full of excitement and fear. This was definitely the scariest adventure we'd ever had.

'Well then?' said Jenny.

'Well then what?'

'Well then, what next?'

'Oh, yes. Er, we need to reconnoitre the situation.'

'Eh?' said Jamie.

'It means we have to have a look around.'

I got out my U-boat Captain's binoculars, and peeped over the broken wall. After a few seconds trying to get the focus right, I could see all around the perimeter to the gate where the Group 9 guy was on guard with his hellhound. Ahead of us there was about five hundred metres of open ground. Beyond that the tower block loomed huge and grim. Between us there were a couple of bulldozers and a dumper truck, left idle for the weekend, plus some other piles of bricks, some wheelbarrows, some planks, and all the other cool stuff you find on building sites.

I checked back to the Group 9 hut. As I watched I saw the guard come out, with Zoltan on a lead. He began to walk away from us, around the inside of the fence.

'A bit of good luck,' I whispered to the others. 'The guard is doing his rounds. Looks like he's going to go all the way round the fence. In a couple of minutes the tower will be in between him and us, so we can make it without being seen.'

'What about sniffing,' said Noah.

'Sniffing is rude,' I replied. 'If you've got a runny nose you should wipe it on a hanky or a leaf or your sleeve.'

'No, I didn't mean *my* sniffing, I meant Zoltan.'

'Well, obviously dogs can't use hankies . . . Oh, you mean he'll sniff us out? Well, the tower should block off most of our smells.

But we should make sure we don't do any farts. It's well known that a dog can smell a boy's fart from fifty miles away.'

'What about a girl's?' said Jennifer, with a funny look on her face.

'What? Oh, I don't think girls do them,' I said.

The Moan laughed. 'Course they do – she does them all the time.'

Jennifer hit him in the ribs.

'Well, you do,' he said very quietly, rubbing his side.

'Maybe she does and maybe she doesn't,' I said, 'but if she does, it probably smells of flowers, so Zoltan won't recognize it. He'll just think, *Oh, what a nice smell. A lovely patch of roses must have come into bloom.* Something like that. But, you know, in doggie language, so it would be more like, *Woof woof, growl woof, snuffle woof,* but meaning what I said.'

Jennifer gave me a little smile when I'd finished. I was being nice to her because we were on a kind of olden-days adventure, and we were sort of knights, so you have to do something called 'being chivalrous', which is all about looking after girls (whether or not they really need it) and saying their farts smell of flowers (whether or not they do).

All this time I was watching the guard and his dog like a hawk. A hawk with high-powered binoculars. Zoltan was the sort of dog that did a wee on every bush to show that he owned the place. So that's how they went.

Walk.

Wee.

Walk.

Wee.

It wasn't long before they'd gone walking and weeing behind the tower. This was our chance. We were out of sight.

'See that dumper truck?' I whispered. They nodded. 'We sprint for that. Ready? Go!'

We jumped over the wall and raced like rabbits for the truck. Jenny got there first, of course. She's so fast she'd probably have got there first if she'd done it in cartwheels.

Jamie made it next, then The Moan, then me, with Rude Word right on my heels, and Noah at the back. I was gasping when I reached the dumper truck.

'Halfway there,' I said, and was about to begin another encouraging speech, when Jenny interrupted:

'Where's Noah?'

Noah. Drat. I looked back. And there he was, halfway between the wall and the dumper truck.

'Looks like he's stuck,' said The Moan.

Noah was lying on the ground, waving at us. His face was crinkled up with pain and fear.

'I'll go back and check on him,' I said. 'You guys wait here.'

I ran back to Noah as fast as I could. There was a big patch of tangled-up barbed wire. Noah was caught in it like a fly in a spider's web. It had snagged his jeans

and torn a great rip in his T-shirt.

'Don't move,' I said. 'You'll just make it worse and probably disembowel yourself.'

Disembowelling is one of the worst ways to go – worse, I reckon, than death by jellyfish, death by parachute-not-opening, or death by scorpions. What happens is that your bowels, which are all the pipes and tubes in your belly, slither out of you like giant worms. You then have roughly ten seconds to re-embowel yourself, which is when you push the pipes back in and sew up the hole, before you die.

Of course usually that's impossible, because the thing that caused the disembowelling in the first place, say a Samurai warrior, a sabre-toothed tiger or great white shark, will still be attacking you, and might well have eaten your bowels in the meantime. Not the Samurai warrior, of course. Japanese people don't eat bowels, but raw fish. They may eat raw fish bowels, but I'm not sure. I'll check on the Internet.

But I didn't mention any of the details of disembowelling to Noah, because then he'd panic and start thrashing around, which is exactly the right way to go about getting yourself disembowelled.

I had exactly what I needed to deal with this situation. I took out my multi-tool. As well as the knife, the scissors, the thing for getting stones out of horses' hooves, the magnifying glass, the hammer, the pliers and the saw, it had some wire cutters.

'I'm stuck fast,' said Noah weakly. 'I don't think I'm going to make it.'

'Don't be stupid,' I replied as I got to work with the wire cutters. 'I'll have you free in a second.'

It was harder than I thought to cut through the thick wire, and I had to use both hands and squeeze with all my might.

But I did it.

First I snipped the wire tangling Noah's legs, and then, more carefully, I cut through the wire caught up in his T-shirt. Each time it made a very satisfying *click* sound.

Click.

Click.

Click.

I thought I'd have made a very good wire-cutting man in the trenches in the First World War, even though that was one of the worst wars ever, in terms of mud, rats, gangrene, death, etc., etc.

It took more than a second, but in the end Noah was free. I snapped my multi-tool together again and put it in my pack.

'Thanks, Ludo,' Noah said as we jogged back to join the others. 'You could have left me there until Zoltan found me and savaged me all to bits, but you came back and saved me.'

'Hey,' I said proudly, 'we're the Bare Bum Gang and we never leave one of ours behind. Unless it is The Moan in one of his bad moods . . .'

Noah looked at me accusingly.

'Only kidding,' I said, and we both giggled.

Chapter Nine

LAND AND SEA OPERATIONS!

'What are you two grinning about?' The Moan asked as we reached the dumper truck.

'Oh, nothing really,' I said as Rude Word licked my face.

'Right, next stage. We make for the entrance of the tower, over there.' I pointed to the big glass doors at the bottom of the building. 'And we have to be quick – the guard will be coming round the side any minute now. Everyone ready?'

Nods from the gang, and off we went

again, running low to the ground. This time I made sure I was at the back so I could keep an eye on everyone.

That meant I was the last to see it.

The others were crouched in a line ahead of me, about ten metres from the safety of the tower.

'What is it?' I asked, but I didn't need an answer.

We were at the edge of the biggest puddle in the world.

There's probably a strict rule invented by scientists about when a puddle becomes a lake, and this one must have been pretty close. It looked brilliant for skimming stones, but this wasn't the time for idle play. The water was thick and brown, and there was a rainbow pattern on it from spilled oil.

'How deep do you think it is?' asked Jenny.

'Up to our necks, I reckon,' I replied. 'Maybe deeper.'

'Can't we just go round it?' asked Jamie.

'No, look – if we go round it the guard will be able to see us.'

I drew a picture in the mud with a stick, explaining the angles. It looked like this:

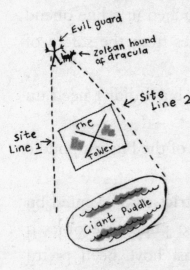

Evil guard

← Zoltan hound of dracula

← Site Line 2

Site Line 1 →

The Tower

Giant Puddle

'So what do we do then?' asked The Moan. 'Go home?'

'Of course not. When you are confronted with a body of water too big to jump, you have three choices. You can build a raft to float over it, you can build a submarine to go under it, or you can build an aeroplane to fly above it. Well, they would all be quite cool – especially the submarine, you know, *Dive! Dive! Dive!* Switching to silent running, firing torpedoes, getting blasted with depth charges, so we have to release oil and bits of rubbish out of the tubes so our enemies think we've been destroyed – all that stuff.

Sadly, we haven't got quite enough time to build a decent submarine, raft or aeroplane. But there is a fourth way.'

'Make your mind up,' moaned The Moan. 'Is it three or is it four?'

I ignored him.

'We can build a bridge.'

I had another good look at the puddle, focusing all my powers on the problem. There was a sort of island about halfway across, made from an upturned wheelbarrow.

'Right then, we need some planks,' I said. 'One to reach the island, another to go from the island to the far shore. Let's get searching. Rendezvous back here in four minutes.' And then I added quietly to Jamie, '"Rendezvous" means meet.'

I was sure we'd be successful. We were in a building site. If ever you need a plank or two, then a building site is the best place in the world to find them. Four minutes later we were back beside the giant puddle.

Jenny had found some sticks, which would

have been handy if we'd been building a bonfire, but they were useless for bridge building.

Noah had some dandelions.

'They're to make the bridge look nice,' he explained.

I found some wire that would be really useful for tying the bridge together.

The Moan came back empty-handed.

Only Jamie found a decent plank, just long enough to reach the wheelbarrow island. Evil plank thieves must have already raided this building site.

I scratched my head and did some more thinking, but this time it was Noah who had the good idea.

'We could use the plank to get to the island, then pick it up and move it on to the other side.'

'You mean we all have to stand on the island together?' gulped Jennifer.

'Standing together is exactly what the Bare Bum Gang is all about,' I replied.

'You're crazy!' said The Moan. 'We'll never all fit on the wheelbarrow. We'll fall in and that'll be the end of us. It'll be like a tragedy on the news: FIVE CHILDREN FOUND FLOATING FACE DOWN IN GIANT PUDDLE.'

'Not while I'm in charge,' I said. 'We can do this.'

I picked up the plank that Jamie had found and bridged the puddle as far as the wheelbarrow island.

Unfortunately, I got a deadly splinter from the plank as I let it drop. I made a small yelp, but didn't cry even a bit, despite the fact that splinters are the most painful injuries you can get (except for disembowellings).

'Let me have a look,' said Noah.

Noah may have been best at rubbing dock leaves on your nettle stings or weeing on grass cuts, but he was also good with splinters. He held my hand and looked at the jagged splinter. It was a very nasty one, right under my fingernail.

'Lucky I've got my medical kit,' he said, and opened his bum bag. It was packed full of dock leaves, but he also had a thermometer he'd borrowed from his mum, and, as he now revealed, a pair of tweezers.

'Be brave,' he said soothingly.

And I *was* brave, not making a sound as he pulled out the splinter. It was at least two centimetres long. Well, maybe one centimetre, but that's still big for a splinter. Actually, with splinters, it's a bit like dog years. So, like, when a dog is four, he's really twenty-eight, and, with a splinter, if it's one centimetre, it's really two. The real menace with a

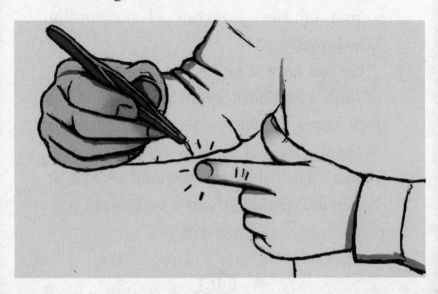

splinter isn't actually the agony you feel, or even the gangrene that dissolves your flesh if germs sneak in. No, the real danger is if the splinter gets sucked into your vein. If that happens, then the splinter will either go straight to your heart, leading to instantaneous death, or get sucked to your brain, resulting in you becoming a mental case and setting fire to your pyjamas, shouting at people in the street, going to the toilet in your pants, etc., etc.

But none of that happened to me, which was a relief, as I don't like going to the toilet anywhere except in a toilet, and certainly not in my trousers. After he got the splinter out, Noah put some special cream on it. He promised it wasn't stinging cream, which turned out to be a small lie, because it did sting, but not very much. At the end he put a plaster around the injured finger.

'Good work, Doc,' I said.

Noah liked it when I called him Doc,

and he smiled a modest little smile.

All better now, I tested the bridge with my foot. It was quite wobbly. And the water in the puddle looked exceedingly deep. And was it my imagination, or did I see a shape ripple under the surface? Croc? Anaconda? Piranha? Who could say?

I snorted at the danger, gritted my teeth and began to walk across. But then I felt a hand on my arm.

It was The Moan.

'No, Ludo,' he said. 'Not you. You've already had a bad splinter. And we can't afford to lose you if you fall in the puddle. I'll go.'

'No, I'll go,' said Jamie.

'I'll do it,' chipped in Noah, even though he was still in a bad way after his barbed-wire ordeal.

I was about to make a speech about how proud I was of the gang and how brave they were and what a noble thing it is to sacrifice your life for your comrades, friends,

Leader, etc., when Jennifer, with a quiet 'tut', skipped across the plank and reached the island. Luckily, none of the underwater predators leaped out to grab her.

'Come on then, you lot,' she said. 'We haven't got all day. There's nothing to be afraid of.'

The rest of us followed her. Except for Rude Word. He decided that he didn't trust the bridge and would rather take his chance with the creatures lurking in the depths, and just splashed straight into the puddle and swam across. He shook himself on the far bank and sat down to wait.

Just because Rudy made it across unchomped didn't, of course, mean it was safe for us. I'd seen a documentary once about wildebeest crossing a river, and the crocodiles always let the first one get across without any bother, and then they'd move in to gobble up the rest of the herd, easy as you or me picking blackberries off a bush.

When it came to bridge-crossing, we boys
weren't quite as nimble-footed as Jenny, so
there were a few wobbles. But we made it.
The island was just big enough for us all
to stand on, if we breathed in and held
hands. There was a minor kerfuffle because
The Moan wouldn't hold Jenny's hand as
she was his sister, and no one really wanted
to hold Jamie's because of where he was
always sticking his fingers, but we got sorted
in the end.

The really tricky part was picking up the
plank, moving it carefully to the other side

of the island, then laying it down across the second stretch of water. Jamie almost fell in, but The Moan grabbed the front of his sweatshirt and saved him, which was the first decent thing The Moan had done for about two years.

The plank didn't quite reach the dry land, but it would only be a small leap from the far end. That didn't worry me much, but what did bother me was that we couldn't get the plank to be completely wobble-free. And everyone knows that there is a big difference between a wobbly plank and an unwobbly plank. It's the same as the difference between a jaguar with teeth, and a jaguar that's had all its teeth and claws taken out by the vet, so all it can do is gum you.

Jenny went first again, running over the plank and jumping the last bit like an antelope. Jamie went next, thumping over the bridge like the opposite of an antelope, say a baby rhino. But he made the leap too. Next went The Moan. He put his arms out to balance, and put his foot in the last bit of puddle when he jumped, but not long enough for a piranha to get him, lethally fast though those watery predators are.

Then it was Noah's turn. I could tell that he wasn't happy. He didn't have a very good sense of balance, and the wobbles really discombobulated him. About three quarters of the way across he stopped.

Jenny and the others urged him on from the front, and I encouraged him from behind. Then, out of the corner of my eye, I saw what I'd been dreading – the guard and his dog were now so far round the perimeter that we were no longer covered by the building. Zoltan was sniffing away at the fence and the guard was looking outwards, but it wouldn't be long before he turned our way, and then we were doomed.

'Now!' I hissed. 'Noah, go *now*!'

My friend looked back at me, his face full of fear.

'I can't,' he whimpered.

There was only one thing for it. I stepped onto the wobbly plank behind him.

'No!' he wailed. 'We'll both fall in!'

But I kept on walking steadily towards him. No matter how carefully I went, with each step the plank bobbed and wobbled more, and with each wobble Noah became more unstable. He teetered and tottered. I wasn't going to reach him in time if I walked the rest of the way.

There was only one chance.

I ran, bounding along the plank, trying to

time each stride with an upward wobble to give me more momentum. I reached Noah just as he was overbalancing. I grabbed his collar, screamed, 'JUMP!' and we both took off.

We were lucky. The plank acted like a springboard, and we sailed through the air. Well, not that lucky. We were going to land in the water. I gave Noah a final mid-air shove and he sprawled out in the mud at the edge of the puddle. I landed a metre short of the edge, splashing down on my feet, but then falling forward. By some miracle, the water at this part wasn't that deep — just up to my shins, and I waded out, wiping my muddy hands on my trousers. My feet were completely brown, as if they'd been coated in melted chocolate.

There was no time to wait for Noah to say thanks. The Quest was calling. We were close to the Grail now, and I felt its power.

'Move, move, move,' I said, and led the

way to the entrance to the grim tower of Corbin, which loomed over us the way a giant sausage would loom over a tiny ant.

Chapter Ten

THE TOWER

There was a set of concrete steps leading up to the glass doors. I ran up them just hoping that the door itself would not be locked.

The door *was* locked. But it didn't matter, because what had once been glass was now just fresh air. Yes, some naughty vandals had smashed all the glass. It meant that we could just walk in.

We found ourselves in what had once been the clean and airy foyer of the tower, when it was new and the world was young and full of hope. Now it was a depressing place, with graffiti scribbled all over the walls, and piles of rubbish everywhere. Plus, it ponged.

Rudy seemed to like it – he ran around sniffing out the rubbish and doing lots of little wees.

I didn't want to linger there. Looking at the faces of my friends, I knew they felt the same.

'I don't suppose the lift works,' said The Moan.

He went and pressed the button a few times.

Nothing.

'Probably a good thing,' said Noah. 'Lifts in tower blocks always get used as toilets.'

'Let's find the stairs,' I said.

It didn't take long. There was a doorway near the lift. The stairs were even more smelly than the rest of the building. Obviously once the lift stopped working people decided to use the stairs as the toilet.

'I think we should leave Rude Word here

to protect our rear,' I said. 'He can bark if the guard comes up after us.'

I explained this carefully to Rudy, and I think he understood. There were still plenty of things to sniff in the foyer, so he didn't mind.

'Up we go then,' I said to the others.

'But we don't even know where in this dump the tramp lived,' said The Moan.

'King Arthur said he lived right at the top, so that's where we go.'

To begin with we ran up the stairs, taking three at a time, trying to leave the foul stink behind us. But soon we were puffing and panting and dragging our tired legs up like old people carrying heavy shopping bags.

'How many floors are there?' asked The Moan.

'Thirteen,' I said back, in between breaths. 'Lucky, eh?'

On and up we trudged. There were windows along one side, letting in a cold

grey light. I kept a close look out for the guard, checking with the binoculars, but I didn't see him or his rotten dog.

As we climbed higher, the whole of my little town came into view. I could see the other, smaller blocks of flats, little redbrick houses of the old estate, and the paler brick of the new estate. There was our football field with the broken goalposts, and next to it the park with its broken swings, broken roundabout, broken everything. Then the wood, with the Valley of Doom in the middle of it. Even with the U-boat Captain's binoculars I couldn't see our den, because it was too well camouflaged, but I knew where it was.

It was magical seeing our world from up here, but also weird and unsettling.

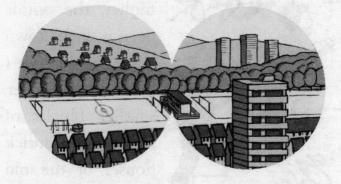

'Are we nearly there yet?' panted The Moan.

For once I didn't blame him for sounding so depressed. It felt like we'd been climbing for all of our lives, and we were only up to the seventh floor. There were six more to go.

'Let's have a rest,' I said.

As a leader, there comes a point when you

have to cut your men (and ladies) a bit of slack. This was that time.

'Anyone got anything to eat?' The Moan asked.

'Only this,' said Jamie, getting out his sausage roll and the scotch egg. 'You can share, if you like.'

But none of us fancied any, so he put them away again.

Jenny was sitting next to me on the highest step, then came Noah, Jamie and The Moan, each one on a step by himself. The rest had helped, but they still all looked pretty worn out. They were grimy and yucky from the sewer and splattered with mud from the huge puddle. Noah's clothes were torn, and I'd never seen Jenny looking this scruffy. Normally her yellow hair was arranged like a volcano exploding on top of her head, but now it was all limp and it had streaks of brown in it from the mud.

She looked at me. 'I hope this is going to be worth it,' she said.

'It depends what you mean by "worth it",' I replied. 'Sometimes you have to do things because they're right and not because you are going to get anything out of it.'

'And sometimes,' said Jenny, her face completely expressionless, 'you really are quite annoying.'

And then she laughed, and I joined in, and so, one by one, not really knowing what they were laughing at, did the others.

'Come on then,' I said. 'Let's finish this mission.'

Chapter Eleven

THE APPROACH
TO THE GRAIL

On we plodded for what seemed like an hour, but which, according to my Spider-Man watch, was only ten minutes.

And then there we were at floor thirteen.

I opened the door from the stairway to the corridor. I counted ten more doors in front of us, five on each side, all painted green.

'Here at last,' I panted. 'We're at the top now.'

'Yeah,' said The Moan. 'It's all downhill from here.'

'How do we know which one is King Arthur's flat?' Noah asked.

'Mmmmm . . . All he said was that it was on the top floor. I suppose we'll just have to check them all.'

'Won't they be locked?'

'Some might be, but not King Arthur's.'

How did I know that? I just did. Call it Leader's Intuition. Or maybe it was just obvious that poor old tramps don't usually have front door keys.

The others left it to me to try the doors. The first one was number 131. I turned the handle but it was locked.

'I could bash it down, if you want,' said Jamie.

I think all the tension had got to him, and he was desperate to do some bashing, and it didn't really matter what got bashed.

'Nah,' I said, and moved on to flat 132.

The door handle turned, and Jenny gasped as I pushed the door open. We slowly entered. But I knew straight away that it wasn't the one we were looking for. The rooms were completely empty, and looked almost as if nobody had ever lived there.

'This is spooky,' said Jamie.

'Yeah,' said The Moan, 'let's get out of here.'

Flat 133 and flat 134 were locked.

'I really don't like it here,' said Noah. 'Can't we just go home?'

'Don't lose it now,' I replied. 'We're almost there, almost there. I can feel it.'

'But what if there's someone else up here? I mean, someone who isn't harmless like King Arthur. My mum says there are bad people around, and I have to be careful.'

I hadn't thought about that. It was true. There were bad people in the world.

But then I looked at the gang. Noah, who may always have been on the verge of tears, but who was clever and kind and my oldest, most loyal friend. There was Jamie, tough, brave, strong. He may have been about as sharp as a marble, but if there was trouble you wanted him on your side. There was Jenny, sporty, fast as a cheetah, the best cartwheeler in the universe, lethal at every martial art. All that more than made up for the fact that she was a girl and had silly hair. Then there was The Moan. Not very fast, not very brave, not very loyal, but my friend.

Together, we were a match for whatever came our way. Apart from, maybe, a full-blown alien invasion fleet, armed with ionic disrupter beams and photon torpedoes. Or an army of robot velociraptors, made out of titanium by an insane scientific genius. But it would almost be worth getting defeated by titanium velociraptors just so I could see them.

It was time for a speech.

'You've all read about the three hundred Spartans who stood up to the millions of Persians at that battle in Greece, the one with the name I can't pronounce. And you know about Captain Scott on his mission

to conquer the South Pole. And remember
in school when we did Geronimo, the brave
Indian chief who fought the might of the
American army for years. And then there's
the good old Charge of the Light Brigade.
Well, that's like us now. We stick together
and we can do anything. Now let's find this
treasure.'

'Excuse me,' said Noah. 'Didn't all the
Spartans end up, er, massacred?'

'Well, yes, but—'

'And Scott and his team froze to death in
their tent, didn't they?' added The Moan.

'Yeah, but you're missing the—'

'And Miss Bridges said Geronimo lost in

the end,' said Jenny. 'And the Indians got sent to rubbish reservations where lots of them died of measles, mumps and rubella.'

'Ah, but not before he'd—'

'And I thought the Charge of the Light Brigade was a disaster. They all got blown to bits by cannonballs.'

That was Jamie. Trust that to be the only fact he'd ever learned at school.

'OK, so they all died. But they live on in memory, and so will we, probably.'

And with that I turned the doorknob of flat 135.

Chapter Twelve

A SURPRISE

I knew straight away from the smell. This was where a tramp lived. A tramp like King Arthur.

'This is the one, isn't it?' said Noah quietly.

In fact the whole world seemed strangely silent. Up here there was no traffic noise, no sounds of children playing, no sounds of life at all.

I nodded.

'Smells of wee,' said Jamie.

Do you think King Arthur always lived here?' Jenny asked.

'No,' I replied, 'I think he moved in when everyone else moved out. Or maybe he lived here years ago before they built the tower, when they had proper houses. That's probably it. I bet he wanted to end his days here, back where he began, just up a bit higher.'

We moved slowly through the flat. From the hall I stuck my head into the kitchen. It was a wreck, with old pots and pans, and broken plates, and cups without handles. It was just the useless stuff that the people left behind when they moved out. I didn't think King Arthur had done much cooking in there.

The living room was bare except for a sofa with the foam padding bursting out, as if it had been blasted with a shotgun. There was a huge stain on the carpet in almost exactly the shape of Africa, which was interesting, as usually big stains on the carpet are in the shape of Australia.

Then we went into the bedroom. This

was obviously King Arthur's Centre of Operations. In fact it looked as though he basically lived in this one room. The walls were plastered with newspapers. I tried to work out if there was something important in the stories, but they seemed to be completely random. Car crashes, foreign wars, petrol prices, silly stories about famous people I'd never heard of. There were more newspapers in stacks in all four corners. There was a bookcase made out of planks and bricks against one wall. It was full of old library books. I opened one. It was stamped to be returned on 9 June 1984.

'He's going to have a very big fine to pay when he gets out of hospital,' I said, more to myself than anyone else.

In the middle of the room there was a kind of nest, made out of blankets, sheets and duvets all piled up together.

'I don't see any treasure here,' said The Moan. 'Let's get out of here before we catch the plague or leprosy or something.'

'Wait,' said Jenny. 'What's this?'

Next to King Arthur's nest there was what looked like a small table with an old tea towel draped over it. The tea towel had a picture of the Queen on it from the olden days when she didn't look like a granny. Jenny lifted up the tea towel. Underneath it there was not a table but a box. The box was made from a dark wood, worn smooth and shiny with time. The lid of the box had a swirly pattern on it made out of the shiny white stuff you find on the inside of seashells.

'Pretty,' said Jenny.

We were all crowded round now, fascinated by the box and what it might contain.

'Open it up, then,' said The Moan.

'Not me,' Jenny said. 'This is your adventure, Ludo, and you should be the one to do it.'

I leaned over and held the lid. It fitted tightly over the bottom part of the box, and the wood was heavy. But despite that it came away smoothly. I put it down gently on the

floor and looked inside. The box was lined with thick red velvet. I touched it with my finger. It was soft and somehow sad.

There were two things inside the box.

One was a book and the other was a big glass pickle jar. I picked up the jar. It was as heavy as a bowling ball. It was heavy because it was full of coins.

'TREASURE!' yelled The Moan, taking it from my hands.

But the smile soon fell from his face as he shook the jar and looked closely at its contents.

'It's all one and two pees,' he said. 'There's probably only a few quid in here altogether.'

'It must be his life savings,' said Noah. 'That's why he wanted it so badly. Poor guy.'

Before I had a chance to say anything, something very strange happened. Rude Word appeared at the door. He had one of those dog biscuits shaped like a bone in his mouth, and his tail was wagging as if he was in a tail-wagging contest.

'What are you doing here?' I said, puzzled. I stroked his nose. 'You're supposed to be keeping guard, you naughty boy. And where did you get that biscuit?'

'Oh, he's not naughty. He's a good boy. Led us straight to you.'

I looked up into the eyes of my mortal enemy.

Dockery.

He filled the doorway, big as an ogre. Then he stepped forward, and the rest of his gang followed him into the room, all of them big and ugly. We were so shocked it was as if we'd been zapped by a paralysing ray, and Dockery reached down and took the money jar from The Moan's hands.

'We'll have that, thanks very much,' he said, passing it back to Larkin.

Then he leaned forward again and yanked my U-boat Captain's binoculars from around my neck.

'And I'll take these as well, as a bit of insurance. You wait here until we're gone, or I'll smash 'em up, OK?'

He said this looking at Jenny. They were all afraid of her because of her tae kwon do expertise. Jenny's hands curled into fists, her knuckles white with rage.

'You're a nasty stupid swine,' she said.

Dockery laughed. 'Stupid? Nah! Reckon you're the stupid ones, leading us straight to the treasure. Good old Larks here heard some of what that loony tramp told you about it, and we thought it was a bit selfish of you to want to keep all that loot for yourselves. We've been spying on you lot ever since.'

'Filthy sneaks,' I said.

'Filthy rich sneaks!' he smirked. 'Come on, guys,' he said to his gang. 'Let's go and buy some sweets, and leave these losers to stew.' Then he turned to me again. 'And remember, you wait till we're out of this place before you move, or I'll smash your precious binoculars into a thousand pieces. If you're a good boy you can come and collect them from our den tomorrow.'

And then they were out of there, cackling and sniggering and slapping each other on the back.

Chapter Thirteen

THE GRAIL

'I always said that was a rubbish dog,' moaned The Moan after they'd gone.

'It's not really Rudy's fault,' I replied sadly. 'He does like a dog biscuit, and we ought to have checked to make sure we weren't being followed. It's something you always have to do when you're on a secret mission.'

'What now, then?' asked Jenny.

'We could tell the police?' Noah suggested.

'What,' said The Moan, 'and explain that we'd sneaked into this place, when it clearly says that trespassers will be prosecuted? Great idea. We'll all end up in jail, and I'll get my pocket money suspended for at least a year.'

'Do you always have to think about yourself?' said Jenny, and I knew one of their special sister-and-brother arguments was going to get started, which usually ended up with The Moan rolling around on the floor in agony.

'Let's see what this is,' I said, taking out the book to try to distract them.

In fact it wasn't a book but a photograph album. I opened the cover. There were ancient black-and-white photos of a child sitting up in a big pram. The next page had pictures of the baby being held by a lady in a hat.

As I turned the pages, we watched the baby grow into a little boy, and then a big boy. There were other children – brothers and sisters, I suppose. And a man with a big moustache who must have been his dad. And at the end there was a picture of a young man in army uniform, standing smartly to attention.

To begin with, the gang carried on grumbling and complaining, but soon they were as lost as I was in the old photographs.

'I don't get it,' said Jamie. 'Why has King Arthur got all these photos of that kid?'

'It's him, you chump,' said The Moan.

'Who?'

'The kid in the photos, it's King Arthur.'

'Really? Oh, yeah, I get it. When he was

a baby. And then when he was older.'

'It's the one thing he's got, from before he was a tramp,' said Noah.

And then it came to me in a flash of golden light.

'Wait, don't you see,' I said. 'This is it. This is the Grail, the treasure. Not that silly old jar of pennies. Like The Moan said, that was only a few pounds. But this . . . this is precious. How can you put a price on a man's memories, on his life? That's why he wanted us to bring it to him.'

The others nodded. Jenny looked like she might be about to cry. Noah already was.

'It's so sad,' he said, a couple of tears rolling down his cheeks.

'I think this might cheer you all up,' said The Moan, who was looking out of the window.

We all went over. Miles below we could see the Dockery Gang. Five little figures.

Running.

They were running because they were being chased.

By Zoltan!

And, right behind him, the security guard, who was waving his truncheon over his head.

They made it to the tunnel just ahead of the dog. Dockery was the slowest runner, and he was the last one in. The dog followed him. I didn't want to think about what was going to happen next. Well, I did really, and anyway, Jamie put it into words.

'He is going to get his butt bitten to mincemeat.'

We all had a good laugh at that.

'But it means we're trapped, doesn't it?' said Noah. 'The guard and his dog, they'll be by the tunnel . . . How can we get out?'

'Actually,' I said, 'I've been thinking about that. I don't reckon King Arthur could have got in and out through that tunnel. He's an old man. He couldn't crawl through there on his hands and knees. He must have used some other way in and out. If we could find that . . .'

We all scanned the fence, looking for the new secret escape route.

'Look over there!' Jenny squealed, pointing to a part of the fence on the opposite side of the tower to the tunnel.

I followed her pointing finger. At first I couldn't see anything. Then I noticed that the bottom of the fence had been peeled back to make a little doorway.

'That's it,' I said. 'Our path to freedom! Let's go, before Zoltan finishes chomping on Dockery's bum.'

'Well, there is quite a lot of it,' said Jenny, which made us all laugh, again.

Chapter Fourteen

THE ESCAPE

I put the photo album back in the pretty box, picked it up and led the way down the stairs.

It was a lot easier than running up, on account of the Law of Gravity, which Jamie once called the Law of Gravy in school, which even made Miss Walsh laugh. At the bottom we crashed out of the doors and ran full speed for the corner with the broken fence.

It was looking good.

We were going to make it.

Or so I thought.

The first thing I noticed was Rude Word pricking up his ears. And then I heard what I been dreading – the distant sound of a savage dog, barking. The others heard it too, and everyone ran faster.

I looked back and, yes, there was Zoltan on our trail. And behind him, as ever, the nasty guard. But the fence and the hole were only a few metres away.

Looking back was my big mistake. First I felt a slight squelchiness. And then I found that I couldn't run. It was as if my legs had been grabbed by some kind of creature that lived in the ground, some sort of earth ogre, say, or a giant spider. Then I looked down and saw it was far, far worse.

I was trapped in the deadliest substance known to humankind.

Sinking mud.

Or, possibly, quicksand.

Somehow the rest of them had all missed

it, but I was trapped, and being gradually sucked down. The mud patch was about as big as the mat you use to play Twister. The more I struggled, the more I sank.

It was a classic mistake.

When you get stuck in sinking mud (or quicksand), you must not struggle but try to pull yourself out using a handy tree branch. But there weren't any. I tried to remember what else you should do.

Oh yes, that was it.

'HHHHHHHEEEEEEEEEELLLLLLLLL LPPPPPPPPPPPPP!!!!!!!!!!!!'

Noah heard and turned. The others were already at the fence. He called to them and they all ran back to me together.

Rude Word was the first to reach me, but rescuing boys from quicksand (or sinking mud) was definitely not one of his skills. He sat down and did a bit of bum-licking.

My legs had now sunk in up to the knees. If the mud reached my waist I'd be as good as dead.

The others reached me.

'Throw me the box,' said The Moan. 'It's making you sink.'

I tossed him the box, and he caught it nicely.

'Give me your hand,' said Jamie, stretching out.

I reached and reached, but couldn't make it.

'That dog's nearly here,' said Noah.

'I know, I know,' I said, trying to control the panic rising in my breast.

I suppose I'd been waiting for this moment all my life. It was the moment of destiny. The moment when I showed what a true leader I was.

'Save yourselves. Just leave me. You'll have

time to escape while he savages me.'

'Never,' said Noah, and the others all grunted in agreement. 'We'll get you out.'

Zoltan was almost there. We could hear his panting breath, hear his pounding hooves. I mean paws, but they sounded like hooves. And the shouts of the guard reached us now as well.

Then I remembered the supplies.

'Jamie, the scotch egg – throw it to Zoltan, it may slow him down.'

With surprising speed, Jamie got the scotch egg out of his bag, took a quick bite out of it – like a US Marine pulling the pin out of a hand grenade with his teeth – and hurled it towards the beast.

As the scotch egg fell, so Zoltan leaped. He caught the scotch egg in mid-air, and swallowed it without even pausing.

'The sausage roll, Jamie, now!'

Jamie threw the sausage roll to the side of Zoltan. It was too tempting, and the big dog swerved to intercept it.

We'd gained ourselves a few seconds.

'Hold my hand,' said Jenny to Jamie. He took it. Then she reached out to me. Noah held Jamie's other hand, the three of them forming a human chain. A human chain of friendship. I touched Jenny's fingertip. Then her hand was in mine.

'Pull!' she yelled to everyone.

But it was too late. Zoltan had scoffed the sausage roll, and his attention was focused on us again. He galloped towards us and prepared to make his killing lunge, with his jaws open, his mouth watering, his teeth at the ready. We cringed, awaiting the monster's attack.

It never came.

At my side I saw a brown blur, and Rude Word sprang into action. OK, more of a waddle than a spring, but there he was, putting his fat body in between me and Zoltan.

The hellhound stopped in his tracks, and

the vicious look on his face changed. He put his head on one side in a puzzled kind of way. Rude Word just sat there. Then Zoltan sat down opposite him. They stretched out their noses and sniffed each other. Then their noses touched.

'I think they're kissing,' said Jenny.

'Yuck!' moaned The Moan. 'That's disgusting!'

'Do you think maybe Zoltan is a lady dog?' said Noah.

'She must be. We'll have to call her Zoltana from now on,' said Jenny.

Rude Word and Zoltana did some more kissing, but the guard was getting closer, and I didn't think being kissed by Rude Word would stop *him* from grabbing us. I could hear him shouting, see the spittle flying from his angry mouth.

'Pull!' I yelled, and they did.

With a huge sucking noise I was free.

'Come on, guys,' I shouted, and we dashed for the fence. Each of us dived through the gap. I looked back and Rude Word was trundling along behind us, casting sorry looks over his shoulder at Zoltana, who also looked sad about losing her new boyfriend.

Once Rudy scrambled through, we all ran away a safe distance from the fence. The Group 9 guard stood there shaking his fist at us.

'And don't you dare come back,' he screamed, 'or you'll be sorry!'

The Bare Bum Gang responded by blowing raspberries, calling him names, etc., etc., until I told them to stop, as he was only doing his job, which involved him being mean to children.

And then, exhausted, we went home, agreeing to meet up the next morning at the hospital.

Chapter Fifteen

THE RETURN OF THE GRAIL

We all gathered round King Arthur's bed. He was in a room with two other patients, both of them old men, both of them asleep. Or possibly dead.

King Arthur looked a lot better than he had the last time we'd seen him. He was wearing yellow pyjamas. His beard and hair had been washed, and he looked properly regal, which means like a king, only posher. He didn't smell of wee at all.

'Who the heck are you lot?' he barked when he saw us.

Actually, what he first said was more like '*Fwap mwap wmap fwap*', but then he reached into a glass on his bedside cabinet, grabbed a set of shiny new false teeth and shoved them in his mouth. Then he could talk properly.

'We're the Bare Bum Gang,' I answered. He looked a bit perplexed at that, which was understandable. 'We helped you when you fainted.'

'I didn't faint. I was just having a little rest.' Then he added suspiciously, 'Are you the lot that were throwing stones at me?'

'No, that was the *baddies*. We're the *goodies*. You asked us to get the Holy Grail from the tower block where you were staying.'

'The Holy Grail? What the heck are you talking about?'

'The treasure. The special thing – you told us all about it. We've got it here.'

I held up the pretty decorated box with the photo album inside it.

His face lit up as if someone was shining

a torch on it. 'My treasure?' he said, almost deliriously. 'You've really got it? Give, give ...'

I passed him the box. He opened it carefully, looked inside, and took out the album. Then he looked inside again. He turned the box upside down and shook it.

'Where is it?' he asked, half puzzled, half annoyed.

'It's there,' I said, pointing to the book. 'Your pictures ... you as a baby ... your life ...'

'But my money? My treasure, where's that?'

'Oh. The money jar. We're sorry, but ... well, we couldn't get it.'

I didn't want to tell him the whole story. It was too depressing.

But just then, I sensed that someone else had come into the room.

''Ere,' said a rough and very familiar voice.

It was Dockery.

What on earth could he be doing here?

He shoved his way between the rest of the Bare Bum Gang to reach the bed. He was holding out a glass jar. A glass jar full of pennies. 'Me and the boys ... well, we had a little think.' Dockery was sort of talking to the air between me and King Arthur, not looking at either of us. 'Felt a bit rubbish. Thought we'd ... well, anyway, here.'

He put the jar down on the bed. King Arthur's bony hands went straight to it, stroking and caressing it like a cat.

'And we added a couple of quid extra,' Dockery continued. 'Buy some flowers or something.'

'Thank you, thank you,' murmured King Arthur.

'Better take these too,' Dockery said, now looking at me. He placed my U-boat Captain's binoculars on the cabinet.

Then he put his big face close to mine. 'If you ever tell a living soul about this, you're history, get it?'

I nodded, and Dockery barged out.

Me, Noah, Jenny, Jamie and The Moan all looked at each other, not even knowing what kind of expressions to put on our faces.

'We should probably go now as well,' said Noah in the end.

'Yeah,' I said. 'I've seen enough weird things for one day.'

We all said goodbye to the king, and left the room.

'That wasn't quite what I expected,' said The Moan, as we walked down the hospital corridor.

'No,' I said.

'He didn't care about the photographs at all,' said Jenny, sadly.

'No.'

'Bit of a waste of time, really,' said Jamie.

Then I realized I'd left the binoculars behind me in the room.

'Back in a sec,' I said.

One of the old guys in King Arthur's room had woken up, and he smiled at me when I came in. My binoculars were still next to the box on the cabinet by the bed. I expected to find King Arthur still stroking his money, but the jar, forgotten, was on the cabinet too.

The old king had the photo album open at the first page, with the picture of him as a little baby in a giant pram. His eyes sparkled and his cheeks were wet with tears.

His lips were moving, but I could hardly make out what he was saying.

'Avalon,' it might have been. 'Oh, Avalon.'

I ran back to join the others. They were outside the hospital by the time I caught up with them.

'What now?' said The Moan, scuffing his shoes on the ground, in a disgruntled way.

'Something fun, I hope,' said Jamie.

'I'd prefer it if it didn't involve stinky tunnels and getting chased by mental dogs,' Noah chipped in.

The Bare Bum Gang certainly needed cheering up. Then I remembered something, and checked my watch.

'Well,' I said, 'I do think we've earned some fun and some excitement. And I know just the thing. Follow me.'

I led them all across town, refusing to answer their questions about where we were going.

It was only when the grim outline of Corbin Tower began to loom over us that they guessed.

'It's today, isn't it?' said Jenny.

'It certainly is.'

'What are you talking about?' Jamie asked.

'BOOOOOOOOOOOOOOM,' said The Moan, right in his face.

'Oh yeah!'

A big crowd had already begun to gather, at a safe distance, to watch the demolition of Corbin Tower. There were quite a lot of children from our school, plus plenty of grown-ups. There were two police officers to make sure everyone stayed where they should. There was one adult I didn't quite recognize, at first, because he wasn't wearing his uniform. And then he winked, and I realised it was the nasty guard, not nasty any more because he wasn't on duty, and he was only horrible to children when someone paid him to be.

The Bare Bum Gang huddled together

to watch, and while we were waiting, I told them about what I'd seen in King Arthur's hospital room.

'So it was all worth it, in the end,' said Noah, smiling.

'We did a good thing,' said Jenny, 'and that's what counts.'

Jamie burped in agreement.

And it was quite funny, because the very moment he burped at least six huge explosions went off around the base of the tower, and it was exactly as if his burp had detonated them. The explosions brought down the building with a massive crash and a great plume of dust and smoke, and I thought then, and I think now, that a really big explosion is definitely the best way to end any adventure.

The Art of Tracking

When you're on an adventure or a quest, such as the one we were on to find King Arthur's treasure, it is vitally important to be able to identify any tracks you come across. Imagine if you were on the trail of what you thought was a harmless bunny, vole or wimpy kid, and it turned out to be a jaguar, yeti or samurai warrior? You'd be in very serious trouble, and probably dead.

When you are following animal tracks you should pay attention to various things. Obviously, there is the actual paw print itself. See if it has big claws coming out of the ends of the toes. If it has, you should probably **RUN AWAY**. You should also note the length of the stride (i.e. how far it is between each step). This will tell you roughly how big the animal is. If the length of the stride is quite teeny-tiny, say two centimetres, it is probably a vole and you are quite safe. If it is medium, say ten centimetres, it is probably a hedgehog, hare or squirrel, although it might also be a badger. You will still probably not be in too much danger, unless it is one of the notorious killer badgers, in which case **RUN AWAY**. If the stride is long, say a metre or more, it is probably a black panther, and you could **RUN AWAY** if you want, but it's probably already too late to save yourself, so you should just hope the end comes quickly.

On the following pages you will see eight different tracks. You have to try to guess what they are. The answers are at the end. I have included the Latin name for each killer beast to make the whole thing even more educational.

If you score **7-8**, it means you are an expert tracker, and could easily live in the wilderness forever, eating wild deer you killed with a bow-and-arrow you made yourself.

If you score **5-6**, you are an okay tracker. You could probably survive for a week in the wild eating rabbits, voles, berries etc., etc.

If you score **3-4**, you are not a very good tracker. You might be able to survive for a day by eating worms and grass.

If you score less than 3, you should never go anywhere near the wild because you will definitely be the one that gets eaten, probably by savage badgers, stoats wolverines, etc.

Of course you can cheat, but that would mean two things. 1) You're a rotten stinking cheater and 2) you'll probably get eaten by a yeti.

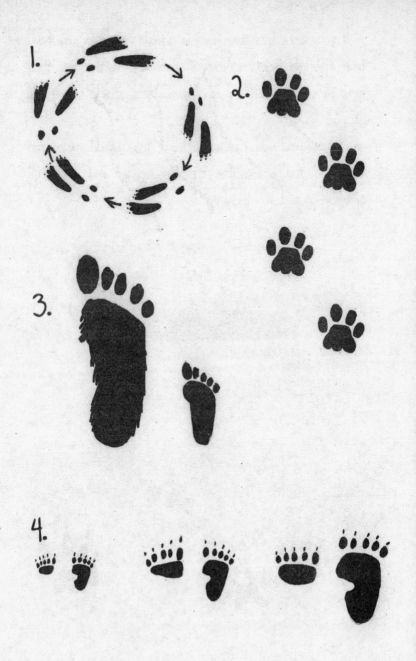

Answers

1. Rabbit (Bunny rabbitus). As you can see, this rabbit is hopping round in circles, probably because it is crazy. You shouldn't eat crazy rabbits, even if you are starving because a) it's unsporting, b) it's silly c) you'll probably become crazy too and hop around in circles like a demented rodent.

2. Black panther (Pantherus blackus). Actually, this could also be a leopard, but I like black panthers more as they are definitely cooler, unless they're eating you.

3. Bigfoot (or sasquatch). Actually, Bigfoot (or Sasquatch) and the yeti (or abominable snowman), have very similar tracks. You can tell them apart because usually the yeti's footprints are in the snow, and Bigfoot's tracks are in the mud. I have put a normal-sized foot next to it so you can see just how big Bigfoot's feet are. This could also be the tracks of a person with one giant foot and one little foot, but there aren't many of those people in the world, so don't waste time thinking about them.

4. These are the tracks of Daddy Bear (Ursus daddicus), Mummy Bear (Ursus mummicus), and Baby Bear (Ursus babicus). On no account eat their porridge, sit in their chairs or go to sleep in their beds, or they'll eat you for sure.

5. Sidewinder (or horned rattlesnake). These are some of the sneakiest tracks in the world, because they don't even look like tracks at all. Sidewinders are deadly poisonous. If one comes for you, your only hope is to squirt lemon juice in its eyes, and then run away screaming while it is temporarily blinded. This also works for baboons, jaguars and piranha fish.

6. Sausage dog (or dachshund). The line in the middle of the tracks is where its fat sausage belly drags on the ground because of its silly little legs. Do not be fooled into thinking you can eat them in an emergency. They are not made out of real sausages, and nor can you make a decent sausage out of them.

7. Wolf (Canis lupus). If you come across wolf tracks you are in quite a lot of trouble. Your only chance of survival is if you're a baby, and the wolf pack adopts you and brings you up as a wolf brother like Mowgli. That is definitely better than being eaten, but on the minus side you'd pick up lots of disgusting wolf habits like licking your own bottom, eating cute little baby deers, etc., etc., and when you grew up you'd probably have to marry a lady wolf.

8. Weasel (Weasily weasily). For their size weasels are the most dangerous predators and if one gets inside your trousers you're as good as dead. For that reason, when hunting weasels, always tie some string tightly around the bottom of your trousers so they can't get in. If one does gain access to your trousers, quickly ask a friend to whack it with a big stick or boulder. This may break your legs but it will save your bacon.